T0367578

GOD'S HITMEN

RENE ADAMS

authorHOUSE®

AuthorHouse™
1663 Liberty Drive
Bloomington, IN 47403
www.authorhouse.com
Phone: 833-262-8899

The following is a work of fiction. References to real people and locations are used fictitiously, apart from the four cross off names-Hussein, Bin Laudin, Gaddafi, and Guevara. The remainder of the work is the product of the author's imagination.

Published by AuthorHouse 03/08/2024

ISBN: 979-8-8230-1564-6 (sc)
ISBN: 979-8-8230-1563-9 (e)

Library of Congress Control Number: 2023918973

Print information available on the last page.

This book is printed on acid-free paper.

CONTENTS

Preface vii

Introduction ix

Chapter 1   The List 1

Chapter 2   North Korea 7

Chapter 3   Las Vegas 11

Chapter 4   Rapist and Murderer 17

Chapter 5   ISIS 21

Chapter 6   The Atlanta Monster 25

Chapter 7   Jeffrey Epstein 29

Chapter 8   Soleimani 33

Chapter 9   El Chapo 35

Chapter 10 Weinstein 37

Chapter 11 Joseph McCann 39

Epilogue 41

PREFACE

Most people today turn to the Criminal Justice System for support in time of need. They expect the apprehension, prosecution, conviction and punishment of the "bad guys". Unfortunately, the system exists for society in general and not necessarily for the individual victim. Too often the guilt is not determined, or if it is, the punishment is not appropriate for the severity of the crime. What happens then you ask? Our system fails even though the police did their job, and the criminal is free to again do the deed. Society is then left wondering how to proceed.

Devine intervention has worked in the past in some instances, but the "higher power", whatever your belief, can also become frustrated and simply tire of some people's ignorance and lack of morals. Typically, the affairs are left to be tended by the people, but if and when it gets out of hand, matters must be addressed. It is at this point the decision had to be made to let mankind act as if they were the right hand of the ultimate overseer. There would be a list made of people to be dealt with and two men would be chosen to carry out the specifics. These men would be known as "God's Hitmen".

INTRODUCTION

The two veteran and now semi-retired cops had been going up the Entiat River Valley for years. They owned 20 prime acres in this pristine Eastern Washington area. It was just up the road from Cooper's General Store, which was located in a small town called Ardenvoir. Their land was somewhat isolated, very wooded and complete with an 1880 log cabin, a barn and a well. It was the perfect spot for rowdy cop parties. The two owners, Ron and Ray and commonly called Ronbo and Raybo, were from Seattle and had been hosting the affairs for years. They called themselves the "R and R" show and they were closer than brothers, having been partners and friends for over 40 years.

Ronbo was a big guy, standing 6'1" and weighing about 210. He was a mellow guy unless a bad guy pissed him off and then he was all cop. He was about 55 years old and he'd been married and divorced three times, all amiacably. He fancied himself a ladies' man, and with a neatly trimmed mustache, he was considered quite a catch.

Raybo on the other hand, was a bit older and was married to his first wife of many years. He was faithful and a good and loyal husband and cop. He stood about 6', weighed about

210, and was a handsome guy too. And he too was mellow unless provoked. He always wore a fancy hat and dressed very well. Both guys were quite the pair and a compliment to the police department.

It was the Thursday before the Memorial Day weekend and Ronbo and Raybo had arrived at their property and had set up camp for what would be lots of cops, wives, girlfriends, guy friends, good food, lots of shooting, and of course, lots of drinking. But before the onslaught, it was time to relax and go down the road to the general store for some "Buckhorn" beer and a "Super Dooper.Cooper Burger", just possibly the best hamburger ever devised. The owner, Chuck Cooper, was an ex-pilot who had been partially blinded in a plane crash and had owned the store forever. He and the locals welcomed the guys while the food was on the grill. It was going to be another unforgettable weekend.

After devouring the food and downing several beers, the guys paid their bill and wandered into the store "for supplies. It was right after walking down one of the isles that everything went blank. No sights, no sound, no feeling, no nothing. The next thing they remember was standing in front of a man dressed in a white leisure suit who stated that his name was St. Peter and that he represented the "Higher Power".

It seemed very peaceful, and the guys were somewhat relaxed as they looked back at the man in front of them. Everything seemed normal but come on! Was there really a "Higher Power" and a St. Peter? Neither old cop put much stock in the hereafter. If there really was a "Higher Power", why did awful things continue to happen and why were there still so many "bad guys"?

St. Peter was clean shaven with salt and pepper hair. He spoke softly, but very well and he addressed the guys by name, which surprised them both. He explained that he was indeed the "welcoming Hand" and that he had a proposition for them. It all seemed quite strange, but unlike the two trained skeptics, they believed him without hesitation. He went on to explain that there had been an explosion at the store. A propane tank had blown, and the ensuing fire had killed everyone inside, including them. He went on to further explain his boss, the "Higher Power", was really getting overwhelmed with crime and corruption on earth and that it had been decided to have mankind itself render assistance. St Peter stated that there was a deal being offered to them both. They could go back as if they had been spared. No one would know. The difference would be that they would be able to move about freely, almost without regard to time as it used to be. Everything else would remain the same except that they would be supplied a list of objectives to be dealt with-bad guys who needed to be eliminated. He went on to further explain that they could decide how to eliminate those on the list. If life in prison was more suitable, that would be fine. Or if death was more appropriate, that was ok too. They themselves could not be killed or even hurt. Transportation and money were not issues. The one overall rule was that they had to follow the list, deal with each person and keep in constant contact with St. Peter. Failure to do so would result in immediate recall and loss of their status. In addition to the list, each man could select one individual of their choice to eliminate, with approval from above of course.

Well, it took only a millisecond for Ronbo and Raybo to analyze and decide their answer. How do you refuse an offer of life after death and an opportunity to get the really bad guys, especially when the offer comes from upstairs. And so, the saga begins. "God's Hitmen" are coming. You are forewarned.

CHAPTER 1
THE LIST

The decision was made; they were given a leather-bound book containing a set of "issues" to be dealt with. It was explained that for the present, there were only ten names on the list. Additional ones would follow as directed. As a precursor, there were four men whose names had previously been dealt with-Sadam Bin Laudin, Sadam Hussein, Muammar Gaddafi and Ernesto Rafael Guevara de la Serna, better known as "Che". A brief explanation followed each name and Ronbo and Raybo knew the how and part of the why the "Higher Power" saw fit to unleash the wrath.

Osama Bin Laudin was first on the list. He was the head of Al-Qaeda and the man ultimately responsible for the attack on 9-11. He was listed as America's number one Public Enemy but had managed to elude his demise for almost ten years. He was one of 52 children of Mohammed Bin Laudin and was born and raised in Saudi Arabia. Islam shaped his political beliefs and influenced his every decision. He was responsible for the 1998 bombings of the U.S. Embassies in Kenya and Tanzania, and he became a follower of Abdulla Azzam who promoted the idea of suicide bombings. Additionally, Osama planned the 2000 attack on the USS Cole, and American destroyer. His focus was simply "acts of terrorism".

Osama's end finally came in his compound in Pakistan, where he had been hiding. He was shot in the head and chest by American Navy Seals. President Obama stated to the public, "Justice has been done".

The second name was Sudam Hussein, the elusive leader of Iraq and their dictator from 1979 to 2003. He had reduced his once rich oil country to a police state by unleashing devastating regional wars, openly stating that he was "destined by God" to rule Iraq forever.

He was proud of his revenge killings, one of which was of 148 Shite Muslim men and boys from the small town of Dujail, just north of Bagdad. He blamed them for a failed assassination attempt on him while he was in a motorcade. Another example was his ordered attack on the northern Kurdish village of Halabja in 1988 in which an estimated 5,000 of his own people were killed and another 10,000 wounded. He contended that he was "firm but just".

When the world, including his own country, finally said enough, Sadam still eluded capture for 8 months. Eventually, however, in December of 2006, he finally faced his punishment. He was hanged and his final words as his body dropped were, "Justice is mine sayeth the Lord".

The third name crossed off the list was that of Muammar Gaddafi, born June 7, 1942. He was the anti- imperial leader of Libya, seizing power in 1969. He "promoted" himself to Colonel and was a devout disciple of Egypt's Nasser. His power was oil and he set out to solve what he deemed were contradictions in capitalism and communism by putting the world on a path of economic and social revolution. He thought he was setting what he deemed to be the oppressed people's freedom. Instead, what he created was a pyramid with his family at the top. His philosophic theory was used to subjugate his entire population. Instead of being a champion of freedom as he claimed, he embodied the opposite. Challenges were met with torture, jail, disappearances and death. Even those who chose exile were often killed by Libyan assassins. Gaddafi was captured and assassinated by gunshot in 2011.

And the fourth cross off was Ernesto Rafael de la Serna, better known as "Che". He was born in Argentina 'where he studied medicine and became a doctor, but soon he learned the "theology of armed struggle and a hatred of the United States.'

He eventually became involved in the Cuban revolt and was even put in charge of the prison at San Carlos de la Cabana. It was here that he carried out numerous executions of those who passed the revolution, summarily ending the lives of many. He instructed his lieutenants: "when in doubt, execute ." His way was based upon the idea that "judicial proof is unnecessary" and must be more of a "cold killing machine motivated by pure hate."

Che eventually left Cuba, going first to the Congo and ending up in Bolivia. Here he made the mistake of thinking that many of the locals would support him and his guerillas. The situation soon turned against him and eventually led to him being captured. After extensive questioning, he was taken into a room where he was shot in the head.

These four eliminations were more than acceptable to the guys and to the world in general. But who had really been responsible for these eliminations? Had there been hitmen before them? Was the military really the force behind this? More questions needed to be answered to find the real truth, which unbeknownst to them and the world, the Higher Power really directed these assassinations. For now though it was back to reality. The "list" was waiting to be dealt with.

Reality Check

Then in an instant, Ronbo and Raybo simply appeared back at what was left of Cooper's store. It was like they had never left the area. The store had really blown up and those inside had been badly burned and injured, but not killed as originally thought. The two old cops, however, were unscathed. Even those inside had no recollection of them being there. Ambulances, fire trucks and sheriffs were arriving and the two guys gave their account of what had happened. It had simply been an exploding propane tank, probably triggered by the store's wood fired grill. After things settled down, the two guys returned to camp and explained what had happened. The party atmosphere was dampened, but things went on through the weekend and then it was back home to the Seattle area.

One of the old cops, Ronbo, had been married several times, but he lived alone in Mukilteo. Raybo on the other hand lived with his wife on Whidbey Island just outside of Freeland. Both were semi-retired because occasionally their police department would call them in on a cold case or for consultation on a current crime. This considered, getting away without arousing suspicion was not an issue. They could simply leave and there would be no questions.

Once the guys were settled and having dealt with the

media about the Cooper tragedy, they got together and looked at the "list" in detail. This was going to be fun-really fun. Imagine, you get to "get" the bad guys and you cannot be hurt in the process. Success is a given. No more wearing the badge like a walking target and relying on skill, instinct, each other and dumb luck to see you through. You get to go in, do the assignment and move on. They were more than ready. They were coming and Hell was coming with them!

CHAPTER 2
NORTH KOREA

Given the world situation, it was assumed that ISIS would be first on the list, but not so. In bold letters was neatly printed "Kim Jong Un", Supreme Leader of North Korea. The reason given was "past atrocities" and to "stop future planned ISIS assistance". North Korea was intending to supply ISIS with nuclear arms. It was also interesting to note that this was what the guys called a "three-fer", meaning that two additional persons were included in the elimination. This was a surprise because not only were two more persons involved, those persons were female. It was Ri Sol Ju, Kim's wife, and his sister, Kim Yo Jong, It turns out they were the real force and firmly in charge-the puppeteeresses so to speak. Both really ran the country. As proof of their power and ruthlessness, it was they who ordered the execution of a woman named Hyron, Kim's girlfriend, and North Korean singer. They had Hyron and eleven members of her band shot in front of their family members. They were also responsible for the machine gun killing of Kim's uncle and entire family. And it was also noted that they alone had inspired the idea of forced labor camps containing 80-120,000 people being held without even a trial. These camps were the equivalent of the Nazi camps of Auschwitz and Dachau. All three, Kim, his wife and his sister, were to immediately be dealt with.

This assignment would be relatively easy, not that any would be difficult. The North Korean leader, his wife and the sister had been off the grid for about a month. Kim had injured his leg while showing off with his military and he and the two had gone up north to his secluded hideaway.

As per their instructions, Ronbo and Raybo let the PD know that they would be out of town for awhile. Then they simply dressed for the occasion, placed their hands on the North Korean portion of the list, and off they went. it was a weird trip at first, sort of like being in a weightless atmosphere. Kind of a tunnel without any sights or sound. And then in a matter of seconds, they appeared outside the hideaway, still fully dressed and feeling fine, as if they had not traveled at all.

The spot was secluded, surrounded by woods and miles from anywhere. Now it was the guy's choice how to do the elimination. It was already established that Kim, Ri and the sister were alone. There were no guards and no one knew their whereabouts. Even the local and worldwide news stations reported that they were thought to have abdicated. And so the guys calmly walked through the main villa gates and confronted the three in the courtyard. They were sunning, and of course, Kim was eating. He looked as if he had gained over fifty pounds since last being seen. Armed with two laser equipped "UTAS" 15 round, 12 gauge shotguns and with their reliable Sig 226, 9mm old duty weapons, the guys confronted them.

It was surprisingly cordial at first, Raybo stating that it was time for a change. Ronbo then explained that a termination had been ordered and Kim would go first. It was further explained that they were no longer in charge of North Korea and that the remaining high ranking officials would soon meet with South Korea and a reunification would be established. Any North Korean threat would disappear forever and the entire region would again be simply known as Korea.

The three started to object and Raybo promptly smacked Kim in the head with the butt of his shotgun. Ri then quickly started to rise but was forcefully told not to move. She complied and was told she and Kim's sister were to watch Kim die a slow death, as they themselves had ordered so many to do in the camps. Raybo wanted to shoot him in his fat stomach and watch him squirm and Ronbo wanted to shoot him systematically in the legs and arms, but both deferred to the method best suited for Kim and the world.

He was "given" a blood clot in his right coronary artery, which caused him great pain at first. He was then asked if he had anything to say, but all he could do was moan. Raybo then watched as Kim's heart began to beat rapidly, causing even more pain but not yet killing him. Both Ri and Kim's sister were asked how-they liked watching someone they loved die a slow and painful death? Amongst sobs, they swore revenge. The old cops just laughed, knowing that would never happen and eventually, when Kim had seemingly endured all he could stand, it was ended with a massive heart blow out. Both ladies then grew silent, knowing that it was now their turn.

They began to try and bargain at first but then quickly turned to pleading for life. They asked for mercy and even said they would repent. The guys said that everything had been decided and that no amount of anything could change it. As far as their country and the world knew they were simply gone. It was as if the ladies had disappeared. But just before they were eliminated, it was explained that two replacements, artificial intelligent folks to be exact, were going back to their capital and that they would be good leaders instead of what they had been. Ri and the sister were then asked if they believed in the hereafter, to which both responded that they thought there were good and bad places. "Guess where you're going?" were the last words they heard as they disappeared. Hell was too good for them.

No trace was ever found of the real sister and Ri. Their bodies were just gone. There were, however, the two replacements that were sent back to the North Korea capital-the two AI'S who would do as directed by the "Higher Power". The people rejoiced that such a change in the couple had taken place. Korea could now be once again united. ISIS would not get their promised weapons and the two replacement leaders could meet as friends with the US President. As for Kim himself, his body was discovered face down in his plate of food. The world would never get to know exactly what had happened to him though because another AI was sent back to the capital as well. Kim's replacement looked good having "lost" the weight and now being much more cordial.

Ronbo and Raybo then were off to Switzerland for a little R&R. Maybe a little skiing, drinking and just relaxing before the next assignment. What a nice and invigorating first trip. After a while, it would be on to Las Vegas where they would gamble a little and then get down to business.

CHAPTER 3
LAS VEGAS

Back home again after their first elimination and a good time in Switzerland, the guys went to their separate houses. Time was not an issue. Both had checked in with the PD and no current cases were in need of their assistance. They even attended the monthly meeting of the "old" retirees. It was simply a time to have fun and talk story. One thing did still bother them both, however. It was an old Snohomish County case from years before. It was a homicide involving a mother and daughter who had gone hiking on Mt. Pilchuck. They both had been shot, stripped and poised. The perp had yet to be discovered, but his time would come. For now though it was back to the list.

In Las Vegas all rules, including morality, can be, and often are, simply compromised. There is prostitution, drugs of every kind, unregulated gambling, rape, murder, underage male and female sex trafficking and on and on. Not to paint too bleak a picture, there is good too, but it's the bad that has attracted the attention of the "Higher Power". This would be dealt with as soon as the guys had a little fun.

They decided to travel the traditional way this time, booking a first class flight from Seattle to Vegas. Once landed, they took a limo to the Excalibur. Both Ronbo and Raybo liked to gamble. Ronbo favored the machines, draw poker to be sure, while Raybo was into the tables with real people, usually five card draw. Well, as you can imagine, neither could lose. One hit all the jackpots on the machine, while the other made the house change dealers at least three times or more. Well after taking their winnings and having one good drink, Ronbo's cell phone rang. It was St. Peter who simply said, "Back to Business".

The name now on the list was Robert Petkavich, an immigrant from the old Soviet Union. He came up through the ranks, gradually becoming the force in town and dealing with everything imaginable that was illegal. He thought himself above the law and was so removed that he had an army for protection and masses to cover his acts and to do his deeds.

Petkavich favored young boys and he had abducted five favorites in his reign, keeping each at least several years until they outgrew his needs. Then it was disposal time and each simply disappeared, leaving their families forever wondering in torment. His latest gig however involved nursing homes. Not so much hurting the old folks, but rather using them to get the drugs supposedly needed by them. Though never proven or even connected, it was theorized by law enforcement that Johnson And Johnson and the Lily Company were involved with him. Only they knew for certain.

The scheme was simple enough. Give the old folks medication to keep them almost sedated–just above the veggie state. Then "doctors" would write prescriptions for thousands of un-needed meds which were then either discarded or sold to foreign countries. Who gets the ultimate payoff? The drug companies who in turn give a huge share to Petkavich. Nationwide, they are talking millions.

And this was just the tip. He also owned a nationwide chain of funeral homes specializing in, you guessed it, old folks. When the old folks died, either naturally or with "assistance", families were encouraged to use his facilities. This amounted again to millions.

Another of Petkavich's predominant issues was his sex slave business. Every major city from New York to Los Angeles, and Seattle to Tampa had his "workers". He would abduct women at a young age, move them to a distant city and force them into prostitution. He would threaten to kill them and their families if they ran. And when they were, in his opinion, used up, he would kill and replace them.

And one final real money maker was his obtaining and selling human organs. You see there is big money for lungs, hearts, kidneys, livers, etc. Because so many people are in need and donners are so few, and waiting lists are so long, people are willing to pay big bucks to avoid the wait and probable death.

Again, his scheme was simple. Employ needy doctors in all states who have health candidates without relatives. Then after comparative blood work and when appropriate, the patient disappears. The needed organs are removed and sold to the highest bidder. And the big profits go on and on. Even his funeral homes would again profit. And so Robert Petkavich, it's your turn.

The guys knew in advance that Petkavich stayed at the Excalibur when in town. He actually owned it and had the top floor "Tower Parlor Suite" as his permanent US residence. Additionally, the really great part was that no one knew he was actually in town. This meant he could simply disappear and it would be assumed that he was somewhere else. What a perfect set-up for the guys to do what desperately needed to be done.

So, hands on the list, the guys simply appeared in the living room of the Petkavich apartment. Surprisingly, the target was in his robe and was looking at the past DVD's of his child lovers, most of whom seemed in early teens. He was startled and immediately turned off the video, demanding to know who they were and how they had gotten there.

Raybo took the lead and relayed their purpose, meaning simply that Petkavich was finished. Everything was pointed out-his using young boys for sex, selling illegal drugs, nursing and funeral home schemes, and the real money maker, selling human organs. Petakavich started to protest and moved toward the bedroom door. Raybo immediately shot him in the leg, causing him to fall. Both old cops quickly explained that his corrupt ways were over and that his empire was finished too. Petkavich asked if there was a way out and it was explained that there was, but first he would have to watch a video. Well he immediately agreed and a video began playing. It consisted of the faces of past, murdered young boys and sex slaves. There were pictures of mutilated organ donners, theft victims and old folks who had been medicated and later killed. Raybo then said, "Here's your way out. In the immortal words of John Wayne, Meet your maker you son-of a bitch." Petkavich was then shot twice in the head,

Clean up was easy. The suite was tided up and secured. Petkavich's body, minus the head and hands, was dumped out the window to the fountain some 35 floors below. DNA was not an issue since he was not in any system, The rest was done when they reappeared magically in the desert. There they burned and buried the head and hand bones. Now finished, they transferred back to the airport and returned to Seattle.

CHAPTER 4
RAPIST AND MURDERER

Now home, it was back to business again, including a brief perusal of the remaining eight subjects on the list. it was now at their discretion as to what order to follow. Would it be ISIS? Or possibly the Syrian leader who had ordered the poison gas attack? Or maybe the person in charge of the diamond mines in Africa? Nah, the guys decided. These could wait. It was time for the long sought after, world wide, serial rapist and murderer. Someone who was a combination of Gary Ridgeway, Jeffrey Dahmer, John Wayne Gacy and Ted Bundy. Someone who was responsible for scores of disappearances, many not even reported because the victims had long since been "gone" due to their occupations-that of male and female prostitutes.

His name was Dylan Janes, a well-known, self-made stock market multi-millionaire. His resources were unlimited and world-wide travel was at his disposal. He hated all who sold their bodies and that was his passion and obsession. He wanted to single handedly eradicate the world of prostitutes. While his goal was perhaps on the minds of society in general, his means were horrifically barbaric and highly illegal to say the least.

Dylan wasn't a bad looking man, but not what you'd call handsome either. His hair was dark and usually slicked back. He was always clean shaven and typically wore a polo shirt, slacks and a thin sport coat. He fancied himself a ladies" man and his money more than made up for any deficiencies. He had a heavy gold chain around his neck, diamond studs in both ears and a large, flashy diamond on the right hand. What a score for the unsuspecting.

His routine was simple; meet in a bar or bistro, depending on the victim's age, and then ask them back to his apartment, be it in Vegas, New Orleans or wherever. Then after a drink spiked with rohypnol, the date rape drug of choice, he would have his way. This typically meant first consensual sex and then on to his real fun-bondage, torturey mutilation, and then disposing of the body in parts in different dumpsters.

In this, his latest, he met a college student who was trying to survive in an Ivy League eastern campus. She had failed a class and being depressed and distraught, had run to a big city where she got caught up in prostitution in order to survive.

In his usual manner, Dylan met her in a bar and asked her back to his apartment, where he prepared their drinks. He was really excited about what he was going to do once in bed. The young lady was trying to be cool, not comprehending what was really going to happen. And then, in an instant, Ron and Ray suddenly appeared in the room. They simply walked in and stated that the party was over.

Well, Dylan was shocked and speechless, but his intended victim, also surprised, immediately rose to leave, not having touched her drink. Ron quickly escorted her and her belongings to another room while Ray "explained" things to Dylan.

After placing and securely fastening the rich guy in a kitchen chair, Ray told him that the game was over. No more "tricks" would be allowed to be disposed of, at least not by him. He tore the necklace off Dylan's neck, threw it on the floor, and then did the same with the earrings and ring. Then to fully illustrate his point, Ray opened the cabinet next to the sink which was full of Dylan's tools of the trade-knives, hand and leg cuffs, electric saws, scalpels, cleaners, body bags, and on and on. He took out one of the scalpels, calmly removed Dylan's pants and then swiftly cut off his testicles and penis. Before the poor bad guy could utter a sound, Ray then quickly severed Dylan's throat and watched as he slowly and painfully bled out. What a shame.

AS for the college student, Ron explained to her that she would be returned to her school and that she would have no memory of failing a class or of prostitution. She would simply appear back at college as if the time away did not happen. She was free from this type of life and she could again be a career oriented college daughter.

Oh yes, and what of the body? Nothing-it was simply left as a reminder of how not to let money lead one to believe they are above the law. The "jewels" were placed on the deceased's body and a long list of past victims was also left so that police could get some closure on open cases.

CHAPTER 5
ISIS

————————◆◆◆◆◆◆————————

Well having put it off long enough to see that ISIS was not going away on its own, it was time to address the current terrorist-two of them in fact. This was going to be good and Ronbo and Raybo get to do a multiple hit-not a "three-fer", but a "two-fer" this time. They would get to eliminate two of the ISIS leaders, maybe not destroying the group, but definitely sending a message.

Just what is ISIS anyway? It was definitely a terrorist group and the guys heard that it had just claimed responsibility for the recent bombing of a 2000- year- old temple in Syria. And there were additional bombings, gas attacks and other horrific crimes around the world. Why? In the name of religion or political beliefs? What kind of religion would condone such atrocities? ISIS kidnaps teens, recruiting them for their army. If they do not comply, they are tortured with shock treatment. If they still do not cooperate, they often have their right arm and left leg amputated.

The first half of the list was decided to be "Jihadi John" as he was called, the infamous masked be- header. Not the real

ISIS leader, but just a "nice gentleman" of English descent who was really enjoying his power and notoriety. Many of you may recall the TV broadcasts of the journalists and other English, German and American citizens who had their heads taken off in front of Jihadi John's group. The guys were really going to enjoy taking this one out.

Finding him was again not an issue. Remember who the guys work for. Jihadi John's real name was Mohammed Emwazzi or "JJ" as the guys decided to call him. He was enjoying his fame in various villages on the border of Iraq and Syria, using women as if they owed him. He feared no one and he accepted no responsibility for his actions because in his own ISIS mind he was cleansing the world and using innocents to get more money and power. He had been a middle class, well-educated young man who had been raised as a boy in Kuwait and then moved to England. it was there where he turned against his country and became a member of the Islamic State.

He was in a remote Syrian village, alone in a small hut. When Ronbo and Raybo appeared, he was a little taken aback. No white men were ever seen free and near him. His English was very good, and he immediately asked who they were and what they wanted. Raybo laughed and told him that it was time for the world to see him as he was and then to be eliminated. He was in a kneeling position, obviously praying to something and he started to rise. As he did so, Raybo took out his large knife and with a single blow, cut off JJ's head. A video was later released to the world showing him before and after becoming a terrorist. His reign of terror was finally over.

The second name on this section of the list was Abu Bakr

al-Baghdadi. He was born in Iraq in 1971 and became the leader of the Islamic State of Iraq and the Levant (Isil). It was he who ordered tens of thousands of Syrians and Iraqis killed by his ISIS troops after they had overrun one-third of Iraq and half of Syria. Just to the east he had been given safe haven for years under the US Coalition forces who were under the control of Abu Ivanka al-Amriki, better known as Donald Trump. Regardless, he was to be eliminated.

Baghdadi was like many of his predecessors who were responsible for things like the burning alive of the "Jordanian fighter pilot, Lt. Kasabeth, or the beheading of American James Foley. (Interestingly, those responsible for those acts had been previously dealt with.)

Baghdadi was easily located in Libya, close to the sea. He had just watched several of his masked men as they stood above 21 Egyptian Christians in orange jumpsuits kneeling in the sand. Having just ordered their execution, he laughed as the beheaded men's blood spilled in the sand and mixed with the waves. It was now Ronbo's turn to deal out the punishment.

Baghdadi is found kneeling and giving thanks to the Islamic State. Ronbo touches the kneeling man who quickly tries to stand but is forcefully driven back down by the butt of a sig pistol. The man then loudly says, "Do you know who I am?". Ronbo replies to Raybo, "We've got another one who doesn't know who he is!". Then he is quickly shot three times point blank in the head and the threat is over. The two guys simply disappear, and the story is told to the world. (Just a note: It was stated that he had killed himself with a suicide bomb in a vest, but his real demise was from the "Hitmen")

While this was not the total end of ISIS, it certainly slowed the terrorist organization down. It was a given fact that the two guys would again be dealing with the group in the future. For now, it was on to an infamous "monster".

CHAPTER 6
THE ATLANTA MONSTER

Not many folks remember the Atlanta Monster, or the Atlanta Child Killer, or the Atlanta Boogeyman, as he was referred to. His real name was Wayne Williams. Even Ronbo and Raybo did not initially remember him, but after reading the report it all came back. During the summers of 1979 through 1981 numerous African American children began disappearing in and around Atlanta. All the cases seemed quite similar in nature. The children were strangled, shot and then left out in the open for discovery. Because of the similarities, it was determined that they were the work of a serial killer.

Wayne Williams was 23 years old and seemed like a normal person on the outside. He was quite the contrary. He was born on May 27, 1958. He graduated high school and soon developed a keen interest in radio and television. He was quite the working man but due to a simple mistake like leaving fingerprints at a crime scene, he was arrested by Atlanta PD and charged with the death of two children. Witnesses even placed him with the two victims prior to their death. He was subsequently put on trial and convicted of two homicides. He was given two life terms to run consecutively without the possibility of parole. It was a relief for Atlanta but not quite justice in the eyes of Ronbo and Raybo.

Williams was quickly located in the Georgia State Prison. He was in solitary confinement due to his brutal attacks on children to try and "protect" him from the other inmates. You see, even bad folks do not forgive or tolerate crimes of this nature. Before being placed in solitude, he was beaten, raped and almost killed. Just a little jail house justice administered by the inmates.

Ronbo and Raybo instantly appeared in Williams' cell, much to his surprise. He was reading a book about traveling the world, something he would never get to do. The guys had the option of killing him, torturing him or simply letting him serve out his sentence. They decided to talk to him before making their decision.

He was cooperative and almost jovial at first, showing no signs of remorse. He did not even ask who they were or what they wanted. He openly admitted to killing the two male victims, and after a little physical persuasion, he admitted to 25 additional killings. He even stated that there were likely more, but that he had lost track. He went on to say that he had twice requested a retrial, was rejected, but still had not given up on the idea.

With all of this, Ronbo and Raybo were fed up and totally disgusted. AS the guys prepared to leave, and after telling him who they were and what they represented, Ronbo had Williams remove his pants so that his manhood was exposed. Then with one quick and circular motion of his knife, he castrated the suspect telling him to "have fun with his bodily functions",

Both guys then left, satisfied that the Atlanta Monster would forever be out of the public and would suffer in jail until his eventual death. It was again time for a little "R n R", rest and relaxation as it were.

CHAPTER 7
JEFFREY EPSTEIN

Next on the list was a well-known American money manager and registered sex offender, Jeffrey Epstein. He was currently residing in New York City in the Manhattan Metropolitan Correctional Center. Thus, no worry about his whereabouts.

Jeffrey was born in 1953 in Brooklyn and was raised in a middle-class family. He was rather intelligent, having skipped two high school grades, graduating at the age of 16. He did not, however, ever receive a college degree. Still, he did get a job teaching calculus at a Manhattan school, but it only lasted two years. After that he obtained a position with Bear Stearns as an assistant advisor and after making some of the big wigs lots of money, he left the firm and embarked on his own financial consulting firm. It was here that it is assumed that he helped clients recover embezzled money and assisted other clients who were embezzlers themselves.

In 1987, Epstein founded a company he called Tower Financial Corporation, which was simply a giant Ponzi scheme. Here he managed to get away unscathed and then went on to other financial investment companies that made him a billionaire, paying no taxes because it was done in the US Virgin Islands. Here he also made friends with many jet setters like Bill Gates, Prince Andrew and even Donald Trump, who is known to have traveled several times on Epstein's private 727 Boeing jet.

His career, while financially lucrative, also had a very dark side-a side that caught the attention of the Higher Power. You see Epstein had a thing for the younger females. He even was accused of sexually abusing many underage girls, some as young as 14, and of having them service his friends. In 2008 he was finally caught and charged with soliciting a minor for prostitution and served 13 months and thus became a registered sex offender. In 2019, he was again caught, this time jailed on Federal sex trafficking of minors. Interestingly, Epstein's long- time girlfriend, Ghislane Maxwell, was convicted in 2021 for sex trafficking and for procuring underage girls for sex, all for Epstein.

It has long been assumed that Jeffrey Epstein committed suicide in August of 2019, but this was not quite the case. When Ronbo and Raybo arrived in his cell, Jeffrey was busy on his computer looking at stock prices. He was rather startled that the visitors had arrived unannounced, and he hurriedly and somewhat worriedly asked them who they were and what they wanted. Ronbo was the first to speak, simply stating they were here to make amends for past actions. Not realizing what that meant, Epstein was promptly hit in the face by a powerful right hand. Ronbo then proceeded to grab him by the throat and began choking the life out of him. just before he passed out, Raybo intervened and placed a bed sheet around Epstein's neck. Then as he looked him in the eyes, Raybo asked him if he knew where he was going. Getting no response, he hit him hard in the stomach and strung him up on the top bunk bed. It looked like suicide alright-suicide by cop. End of story for Epstein.

For now, it was on to the next mission. This time in the middle east and with someone named Qasem Soliemani, Iran's formidable General. First though, it was once again party time and time for some fun. Maybe in Italy for some wine time!

CHAPTER 8
SOLEIMANI

Italy was fun, to say the least. Ronbo got hooked up with a nice lady who showed him the famous wine chateau and then took him to her place for a night of fun. Ronbo liked new ladies and he was more than ready for action. Raybo on the other hand just amused himself with lots of spirits and then settled down for a quiet night of foreign television and much needed solitude. He also thought a lot about his wife and what he would do when home time came around. Both men had a good time, and both were ready for the commander of the Quds Force, Qasem Soleimani, nicknamed The Shadow Commander.

In the late 1990s Soleimani became the real leader of the Quds Force, the external wing of Iran's Islamic Military Guard. A year earlier the Trump Administration named this unit a terrorist organization which I prompted Soleimani to issue a public threat to the United States. He said, "If you start a war, we will end it!". Soleimani was considered to be the second most powerful man in Iran, many referring to him as its future president.

Soleimani was 62 years old, sort of a quiet man who traveled by airplane and on the ground via a motorcade. He thought himself invincible. Later in life he shook off the secrecy and almost relished in the attention. This made him highly visible to his enemies, namely the United States. He was amongst the most well- known personalities in Iran, viewed by some as a hero and by others as a murderer.

During the last few days of December 2019, there were many rocket attacks and air strikes against both Iran and Iraq. On December 31st protesters stormed the US Embassy chanting, "Death to America!". Finally on January 3rd of 2020 a drone strike was ordered by President Trump on a convoy carrying Soleimani from the Bagdad airport. The General was consequently killed, his wrecked car seen smoldering on television with his dead body inside.

Unbeknownst to all, Ronbo and Raybo played a significant part in the attack. You see it was they who guided the drone attack that killed Soleimani. The act itself was done and the US took full responsibility. Now there was much protesting and fighting. Who would now be in charge? What was to be done? Iran's military was humiliated both at home and abroad and for now the Iranian Regime was on hold, but everyone knew that it was only temporary. Now it was back to the list and on to the next target. His name was El Chapo.

CHAPTER 9
EL CHAPO

$\leftrightarrow\leftrightarrow\leftrightarrow\leftrightarrow\leftrightarrow\leftrightarrow$

El Chapo's real name is Joaquin Guzman He is said to have controlled the North American and Australian drug markets and has allegedly killed over 100,000 people. He was a former drug lord and former leader of the Sinaloa Cartel, an international drug syndicate in Mexico.

Bom in 1957 and raised by an abusive father in a poor farming family. He was introduced to the drug trade by his dad by raising marijuana to sell to local drug dealers. He founded his own drug cartel in 1983 and began to supply not only marijuana but also methamphetamine and cocaine. He rapidly became the largest dealer in the world, pioneering the use of distribution cells and using long range tunnels near the border of the United States. His wealth was estimated to be the same as Pablo Escobar. El Chapo is said to have had at least 4 wives and claims to have at least 11 children, one of which is continuing the drug business. In fact. it is assumed that most of his family is still in the drug business. Maybe some of them will be on the future "list".

El Chapo has been arrested at least three times, the last of which he was captured in Mexico following a shootout and was subsequently extradited to the U.S. Here he was tried and convicted of several crimes including drug distribution, conspiracy, use of a firearm to further drug distribution, money laundering and on and on. He was sentenced to life in prison without the possibility of parole plus 30 years. Additionally, he forfeited more than 12.6 billion dollars in assets. He is currently incarcerated in Colorado, where he has been since 2016.

Ronbo and Raybo were responsible for his capture, and they knew it was their turn for justice. They led the Mexican authorities to him and made sure that the shootout did not harm him. Now in Colorado, they met him in his prison cell. The two guys knew the warden from before because he had previously been the warden of a Washington State prison. They therefore immediately got approval to keep El Chapo in solitary confinement forever. This would be sufficient punishment for him. The guys didn't even hit him. He was simply left to his own demise.

Now it was on to another infamous man-a sex offender named Harvey Weinstein.

CHAPTER 10
WEINSTEIN

———————— ✦✦✦✦✦ ————————

Harvey Weinstein was born in New York City in 1952. He is a convicted sex offender and has been also convicted of other serious crimes including rape. He was a film producer until 2017 when he was charged and later convicted of rape. He is considered a sexual predator. Ronbo and Raybo wanted more information on him, and they delved into his past.

Weinstein's net worth is reportedly 25 million dollars, which leads to part of his defense. He says that many women are simply after his money. More then 80 women have accused him of sexual misconduct, allegedly occurring over decades. He stood trial in both New York and Los Angeles and was found guilty in both for rape and other sexual acts. Both the New York Times and the New Yorker have published reports of his decades of sexual harassment and assault. The movie mogul had been doing his dirty work as far back as the 80's and continued until his victims decided enough was enough.

Weinstein was sacked by the board of his company in 2017 "in light of new information about his misconduct". Numerous women, including Gwyneth Paltrow and Angelina

Jolie, came forward and accused him of forcible rape and sexual harassment. The United Kingdom is currently investigating specific allegations against Weinstein. His current wife, Georgina Chapman, announced she was leaving him, saying her priority was her young children. This unfolded in 2017.

In 2018 and on to current time, Weinstein continues to face allegations of sexual misconduct, sexual assault and rape. He is currently incarcerated at the Twin Towers Correctional Facility in Los Angeles where he will likely spend the rest of his life-18 to 24 years. Then, assuming he survives, it's back to New York to serve out the remaining 21 years of his sentence there. in addition to this all, he is the subject of numerous civil lawsuits regarding his past actions.

The guys were perplexed to say the least. Weinstein was being punished for his crimes during the past decades simply by being in jail. He was no longer a threat to women, and he would not ever be a free man again, even if by some miracle he won an appeal in Los Angeles.

Ronbo and Raybo just instantly appeared in his cell and after the introductory formalities, stated that they were just checking that he was where he was supposed to be. Before he could say anything, the guys simply left. They did, however, make certain that Weinstein would spend the rest of his life not only in jail, but confined to a wheelchair. Just a little added penalty for him to enjoy.

Enough of this. Now it was on to the final person on the list, another out of the country man named Joseph McCann.

CHAPTER 11
JOSEPH MCCANN

The two guys did not remember being in the United Kingdom before their current mission. It was quite an experience seeing the traffic in London and all the tourist sights. Ronbo and Raybo enjoyed their city time, but it was now time for a man named Joseph McCann

McCann was young, 34 to be exact. He had been in trouble with the law before having been convicted for burglary while armed with a knife in 2008. Shortly after his arrest, however, he was released despite being subject to imprisonment for a public protection sentence. He was again arrested for burglary and theft in 2017 and was again paroled. This was an error by the Ministry of Justice, an event that would haunt the system forever.

In 2019 McCann was arrested for the final time. This time the crimes included murder, kidnapping and rape, including that of an 11-year-old boy and a 7dyear-old woman. Ronbo and Raybo were baffled as to why the man had been freed. He was a menace to society and had to be dealt with.

At any rate McCann was tried and convicted of this horrific

series of crimes and was sentenced to 33 life sentences. He would forever be incarcerated, but what to do with him in the meantime.

After much deliberation, it was decided to simply pay him a visit. The prison officials had admitted and apologized for failings in his release. One staff member had even been demoted and admitted, after an internal investigation, that it was partially due to cuts in the justice system.

Anyway, the guys simply appeared in McCann's cell. He was alone due to the seriousness of his crimes; not with the general population because he would likely be tortured and killed. Ronbo was first to acknowledge the criminal and began by telling him several times what a low life he was. This was after smacking him several times and kicking him hard in the groin. Raybo waited while the "victim" dealt with the pain and then he too hit McCann, leaving numerous marks.

It was now time for the final punishment. Joseph McCann would be released into the general population to serve his sentences. The guys cleared it with the high prison officials and it was done. Joseph McCann was with the bad guys who would deal with the final punishment.

Now it was it was time for Ronbo and Raybo to relax and have a real vacation, but first they had to again meet with St. Peter for more instructions.

EPILOGUE

The two men were almost immediately in front of St. Peter who was again dressed all in white. He immediately went on about what a great job the guys were doing and how the Lord appreciated all the help they were giving. There was one thing that the Lord wanted them to do. They were to choose two additional "old cops" to assist in their work. They could even choose someone who had already passed. But it was decided they needed the help because crime and bad guys were on the rise. St. Peter then asked if there were any questions.

Ronbo and Raybo quickly agreed that they would gladly choose two additional guys to help with the "cleansing". The one thing on their minds was this: Why does God allow bad things to happen to good people and why does he allow bad people to exist and do bad things? St. Peter was somewhat taken aback but he did have a response. It was simply that God was tired of handling all that happens on Earth. God is tired of mass shootings, natural disasters and illnesses and disease that take countless innocent lives. This is why God has asked for your help. Help the children who have nothing and who are tortured on earth. And help those who do not deserve punishment. This is why you have been chosen to do what you can. Go forth and do good. It is Gods will.

And so the guys will choose two more to help with the tasks. Who will they be? And who will get eliminated? And were there other "old cops" or former helpers? One thing for sure, one of their choices to deal with will be those responsible for the Pilchuck murders of a mother and daughter because it's so brutal and because it's close to home-Mukilteo and Whidbey Island, both in Washington State. But enough for now. It's vacation time.

Printed in the United States
by Baker & Taylor Publisher Services